Dear Parent:
Your child's love of readir

Every child learns to read in a different v
speed. Some go back and forth between
favorite books again and again. Others re
order. You can help your young reader improve and become more
confident by encouraging his or her own interests and abilities. From
books your child reads with you to the first books he or she reads
alone, there are I Can Read Books for every stage of reading:

SHARED READING
Basic language, word repetition, and whimsical illustrations,
ideal for sharing with your emergent reader

BEGINNING READING
Short sentences, familiar words, and simple concepts
for children eager to read on their own

READING WITH HELP
Engaging stories, longer sentences, and language play
for developing readers

READING ALONE
Complex plots, challenging vocabulary, and high-interest topics
for the independent reader

ADVANCED READING
Short paragraphs, chapters, and exciting themes
for the perfect bridge to chapter books

I Can Read Books have introduced children to the joy of reading
since 1957. Featuring award-winning authors and illustrators and a
fabulous cast of beloved characters, I Can Read Books set the
standard for beginning readers.

A lifetime of discovery begins with the magical words "I Can Read!"

Visit www.icanread.com for information
on enriching your child's reading experience.

DISNEY

MEET THE ROBINSONS

Journey to the Future

Meet the Robinsons: Journey to the Future Copyright © 2007 Disney Enterprises, Inc. All rights reserved. No part of this book may be used or reproduced in any manner whatsoever without written permission except in the case of brief quotations embodied in critical articles and reviews. Printed in the United States of America. For information address HarperCollins Children's Books, a division of HarperCollins Publishers, 1350 Avenue of the Americas, New York, NY 10019. www.icanread.com
ISBN-10: 0-06-112472-9 — ISBN-13: 978-0-06-112472-3

❖   First Edition

I Can Read!

READING **2** WITH HELP

DISNEY
MEET THE ROBINSONS
Journey to the Future

Adapted by Apple Jordan

Illustrated by Alan Batson, Andrew Phillipson, and
The Disney Storybook Artists

Designed by Disney Publishing's Global Design Group

HarperCollins*Publishers*

Lewis was 12 years old.

He loved inventing things,

but they did not always work.

"Oops!" he said

as his newest invention failed.

"I was trying to make sandwiches!"

Lewis was upset.

He never wanted to invent again.

One day, Lewis met a boy
named Wilbur Robinson.
Wilbur was from the future.
"Hi, Lewis!" said Wilbur.
"Do you want to visit the future?"

"I have a Time Machine!"

Wilbur said.

"Right. Sure," Lewis replied.

Lewis did not believe Wilbur,

so Wilbur pushed Lewis off the roof.

Lewis landed on a Time Machine!
Wilbur jumped in after Lewis.
"Wow!" said Lewis. "This is cool!"
The Time Machine was red,
and it had a clear roof
that looked like a bubble.

"Where are we going?" Lewis asked.

"To the future!" exclaimed Wilbur.

He pressed a button,

and the Time Machine took off.

The Time Machine flew into the sky.

"Ahhh!" Lewis screamed.

"We are going very fast!"

Outside the window,

Lewis saw a burst of color.

When the Time Machine slowed down,

Lewis looked outside again.

He saw a big, clean, shiny city.

"Wow!" said Lewis. "The future!

It is possible to travel in time."

"Hey!" said Lewis. "Look at that!

That man is floating in a bubble!"

Wilbur smiled.

"People travel in bubbles," he said.

The boys soon landed
on Wilbur's front lawn.
They bounced on the grass.
"This is great!" Lewis shouted.
"My dad invented bouncy grass,"
Wilbur said.
Lewis laughed and bounced
as high as he could.

Lewis met a robot in the garage.

"My name is Carl," the robot said.

"I can do lots of things.

Look at my flags and fireworks!"

Then Wilbur and Carl left,

and Lewis got sucked up

into a Travel Tube by mistake.

"Yikes!" shrieked Lewis.

The wind pushed Lewis along so fast

that he couldn't stop!

Finally Lewis shot out of the tube.

When he stood up,

he heard a loud noise.

It was a speeding train!

Aunt Billie invented fast model trains.

Lewis looked inside a cannon.

Suddenly a man popped out.

"Hi there!" said Uncle Gaston.

He invented lots of different cannons.

Lewis found Carl in the kitchen.

His chest sprang open.

Little robots jumped out of Carl.

They looked just like him.

The mini-Carls helped Carl
make dinner.
It wasn't hard.
In fact, it was fun!

""Hey! Look!" said Wilbur.
"There is Uncle Art's spaceship!
He delivers pizza to everyone
in outer space."

Lewis met the rest
of Wilbur's family at dinner.
They were all inventors.

We all failed before we succeeded,"

they said.

"You have to keep trying.

One day your inventions will work."

Carl came back to the dining room.

He had a sandwich maker.

"I invented one of those,

but it broke," Lewis said sadly.

This sandwich maker broke, too.

Could Lewis fix it?

Lewis could not fix it.
Peanut butter and jelly
splattered all over everyone.

"Hooray!" the Robinsons cheered.

"That was a good effort!

You must keep trying.

Then you can make a better invention!"

Lewis cheered up.

"That makes sense," he said.

It was time to go.

The boys zoomed off

in the Time Machine.

"Just keep trying,"

Wilbur reminded Lewis.

Lewis felt better now.

He was going to keep moving forward!

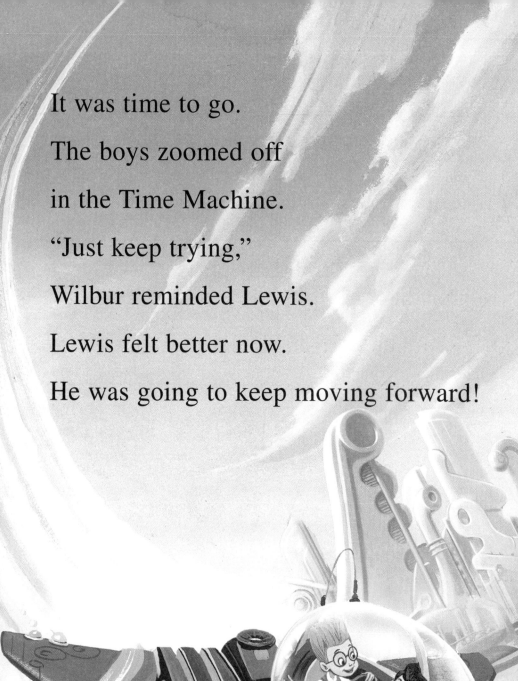